Curious George

Goes to the Hospital

by
Margret & H. A. Rey

IN COLLABORATION WITH THE CHILDREN'S HOSPITAL MEDICAL CENTER, BOSTON

HOUGHTON MIFFLIN HARCOURT

Boston New York

Other Books About Curious George by H. A. Rey:

Curious George

Curious George Gets a Medal

Curious George Rides a Bike

Curious George Takes a Job

Curious George Learns the Alphabet

and for beginning readers:

Curious George Flies a Kite by Margret Rey;

    illustrated by H. A. Rey

Copyright assigned to Houghton Mifflin Harcourt Publishing Company in 1993

Library of Congress catalog card number: 65-19301

ISBN 978-0-395-18158-4 hardcover

ISBN 978-0-395-07062-8 paperback

For information about permission to reproduce selections from this book,
write to Permissions, Houghton Mifflin Harcourt Publishing Company,
215 Park Avenue South, New York, New York 10003.

Printed in China

SCP 70 69

4500585201

This is George.

He lived with his friend, the man with the yellow hat. He was a good little monkey, but he was always curious.

Today George was curious about the big box on the man's desk.

What could be in it? George could not resist.
He simply HAD to open it.

It was full of funny little pieces of all sorts of
shapes and all sorts of colors.

George took one out.
It looked like a
piece of candy.

Maybe it WAS candy. Maybe he could eat it.
George put the piece in his mouth—and before
he knew, he had swallowed it.

A while later the man with the yellow hat came home. "Why, George," he said, "I see you have already opened the box with the jigsaw puzzle. It was supposed to be a surprise for you. Well, let's go to work on it."

Finally the puzzle was finished—
well, almost finished.
One piece was missing.

The man looked for it everywhere, but he could not find it. "That's strange," he said, "it's a brand-new puzzle. Well, it cannot be helped. Maybe we'll find it in the morning. Let's go to bed now, George."

The next morning George did not feel well. He had a tummy-ache and did not want to eat his breakfast.

The man was worried. He went to the telephone and called Doctor Baker. "I'll be over as soon as I can," said the doctor.

First Doctor Baker looked down George's throat and felt his tummy. Then he took out his stethoscope and listened. "I'm not sure what's wrong," he said. "You'd better take George to the hospital and have an X-ray taken. I'll call them and let them know you are coming."

"Don't worry, George," said the man when they were driving to the hospital, "you have been there before, when you broke your leg. Remember how nice the doctors and nurses were?"

George held his big rubber ball tight as they walked up the hospital steps.

A nurse took them down a long hallway to a room where she gave George something to drink that looked white and tasted sweet. "It is called barium," the nurse explained. "It helps the doctors find out what is wrong with you, George."

In the next room stood a big table, and a doctor was just putting on a heavy apron. Then he

gave the man one just like it. George was curious: Would he get one too? No, he did not.

"You get on that table, George," the doctor said. "I am going to take some X-ray pictures of your insides." He pushed a button and there was a funny noise. "There—now you may get up, and we will have the X-rays developed right away."

"Now let's see . . . There is something there that should not be," said the doctor when they were looking at the X-rays.

"Why, that looks like . . . I think that must be the piece that was missing in our jigsaw puzzle yesterday!" said the man. "Well, well, well," said the doctor, "at least we know now what is wrong with our little patient. I'll tell Doctor Baker right away. George will have to stay at the hospital for a few days. They'll put a tube down his throat to get the piece out. It's only a small operation. I'll call a nurse and have her take you to the admitting office."

Many people were waiting outside the office. George had to wait too.

"Look, Betsy," the woman next to him said to her little girl, "there is Curious George!" Betsy looked up for a moment, but she did not even smile. Betsy had never been to a hospital before. She was scared.

Finally it was George's turn.

A pretty young nurse took him to the next room —my, how many rooms and how many nurses there were! One nurse wrote down a lot of things about George: his name and his address and what was wrong with him. Another nurse put a bracelet around his wrist. "It has your name on it, George," she said, "so that everybody knows who you are."

Then the pretty young nurse came back. "My name is Carol," she said. "I am going to take you to your room now—we call it the children's ward—and put you to bed. There will be lots of children to keep you company."

And so it was. There were a lot of children in the room. Some were up and around; others were in their beds, with a doctor or a nurse looking after them.

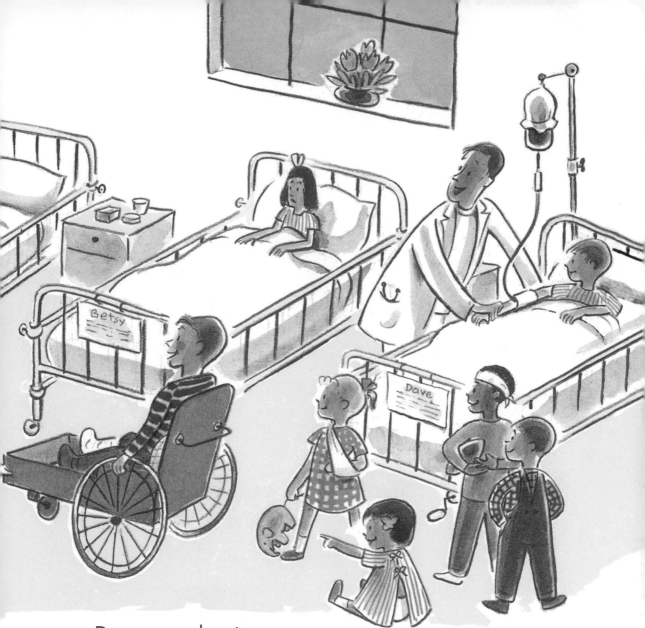

Dave was having a
blood transfusion. Steve had his leg bandaged
and was sitting in a go-cart. Betsy was in bed
looking sad. George got the bed next to Betsy.

George was glad when he
was in his bed at last. His tummy
was hurting again.

The man sat with him for a while. "Now I have
to leave you, George," he finally said. "I'll be
back first thing in the morning before they take you
to the operating room.
Nurse Carol will tuck
you in when it's time
to sleep."

Then he left. George
just sat there and cried.

As he had promised, the man was back early
next morning. The nurses were keeping George
very busy. One nurse was taking his tempera-
ture; one was taking his blood pressure; one
was giving him a pill ("To make you sleepy,
George," she said), and one
was getting ready
to give him
a shot.

"It's going to hurt, George," she said, "but only for a moment."

She took his arm, and George let out a scream.

"But the needle hasn't touched you yet," said the nurse, laughing. "There—now it's done. That wasn't so bad, was it?"
No, it really was not.
And anyway, it was over now.

By the time the attendant came with the stretcher
to wheel him to the operating room, George was
getting sleepy. He tried
hard to stay awake.
He was curious to see
what would happen next.

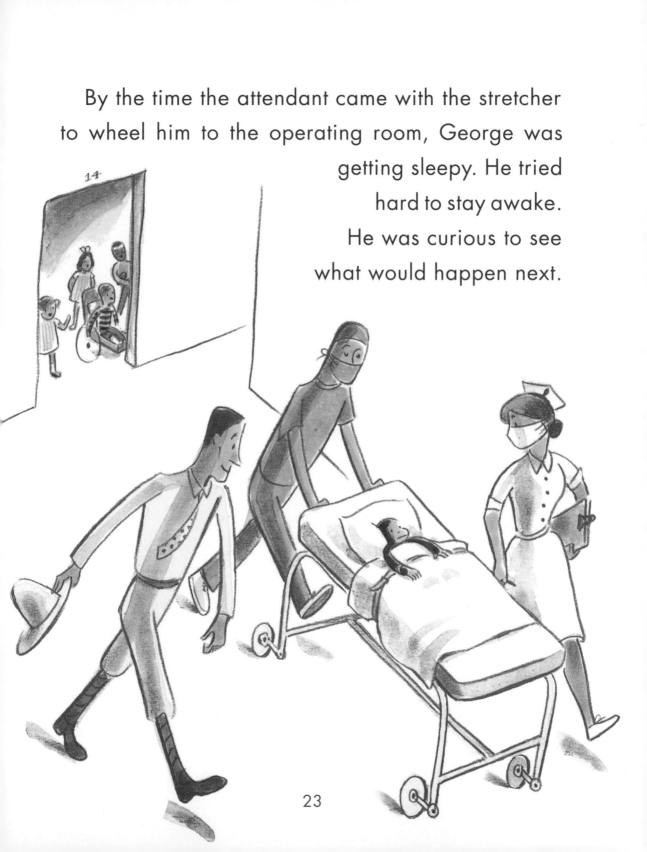

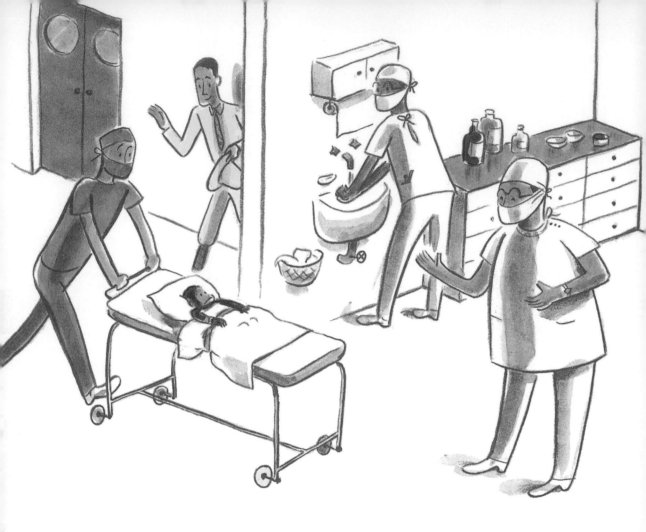

He could see a big table with bright lamps over it and doctors and nurses all around. They had caps on their heads and masks over their faces; only their eyes were showing.

One of the doctors winked at George and patted his head. It was Doctor Baker, who had

been to the house when it all had started. He looked funny with his mask on . . . And then George was fast asleep.

When George woke up he did not know what had happened. He did not even know where he was. Then he saw Nurse Carol. "It's all done, George," she said. "They got the piece out. In a day or two you will be running around again."

The man had brought him a picture book. But George felt sick and dizzy. His throat was hurting, too. He was not even curious about the new book. He closed his eyes again. "We'll let him sleep," said Nurse Carol. "The more he sleeps, the better."

The next morning George felt better. He even ate a dish of ice cream. Dr. Baker came to see him, and the man, of course, came too.

Betsy was watching him from time to time. She seemed a little less sad, but she still did not smile.

Steve wheeled his go-cart over to George's bed. "Tomorrow I can get up and try to walk," he said. "Boy, I can hardly wait."

"I'll take you to the playroom now, George,"
Nurse Carol said the next morning, "and in the
afternoon your friend will come and take you
home."

The playroom was full of children. A lady was
showing Betsy how to use finger paint. There were
all sorts of things to play with, even a puppet
theater—and that was just the thing for George.
He had four hands so could handle four puppets
at the same time.

George gave
a real puppet show,
with a dragon
and a clown
and a bear
and a policeman.

The children laughed
and shouted,
and even Betsy
for the
first time
smiled a little.

29

There was a TV set in the playroom and also a
record player. George was curious: If he climbed
on the record player
and turned the switch,

would it go round
and round like a
real merry-go-round?

It did!
It started slowly,
then it went faster and
faster, and whoopee!
George had lost his
balance and was
sailing through the air . . .

Luckily George landed on a soft cushion. The children cheered, and Betsy smiled again. George was SO funny.

But then the play lady picked George up. "That's enough for now," she said. "You'd better take a nap before lunch. We have a big day ahead of us. The mayor is coming to visit the hospital today, and later on you will be going home, George."

When George woke up,
Steve was just taking his first steps.
A nurse was helping him, and the children were
watching.
The go-cart was standing there empty.
George was curious.
He looked at it.
Then he climbed
into it.

Then he grabbed
the wheels and then, while
nobody was looking, he wheeled the go-cart right
out of the room.

George
could make
the go-cart go very fast.
This was fun! Down the hall he went.
By now the nurse had noticed that he
was gone and came running after him.
"George! George!" she shouted.

But George was
too excited to listen.
He wheeled around the corner
and down the ramp to the floor below,
where some men were busy pushing
lunch carts, and a lot of doctors and

nurses were showing the mayor around.

George tried to stop,
but it was too late.
WHAM!—the go-cart landed
right in the middle of everything.
Lunch carts tumbled. Spinach and scrambled
eggs and strawberry jam were all over the floor.
People fell over each other, and George was
thrown out of the go-cart and landed right in
the mayor's arms.

What a mess it was!

"You broke all my dishes!" someone cried.

"He ruined the go-cart!" complained another.

"What will the mayor think of it?" whispered
someone else. And so it went.

Suddenly everybody looked up and listened.
From above came happy laughter—and there
stood Betsy, laughing, laughing, laughing. Then
the children joined in, then the mayor started
laughing, and finally everybody just laughed and
laughed. Everybody, that is, except George.

Betsy came running down the ramp, threw her arms around George, and kissed him. "Don't be sad, George," she said. "The whole thing was SO funny! I never laughed so much in my life. I'm so glad you were in the hospital with me."

Now the director of the hospital spoke: "I am sorry this happened, Mr. Mayor," he said, "but I think we'll just clean up the mess and be done with it."

"George," he went on, "you've made a terrible mess. But you also made our sad little Betsy happy again, and that is more than any of us has done.

"And now I see your friend has just come to take you home. So, goodbye, George, and take good care of yourself."

The children
crowded around the
windows waving goodbye when
George and the man with the yellow
hat were finally leaving the hospital.

As the car was
turning into the driveway
Nurse Carol came running after them. "Here's
a little package with something that belongs to
you, George," she called. "But don't open it before you are home!"

George was curious—
well, who would not be?
The moment he reached home
he ripped the paper off,
tore open the box—
and THERE

was the piece
of the puzzle
that had caused
all the trouble!

"How nice of the doctor to save it for us!" said
the man with the yellow hat. "And NOW we can
finish the puzzle."

The End